In the Ice Caves of Krog

A Magical World Awaits You
Read

THE SECRETS OF DROON

In the Ice Caves of Krog

by Tony Abbott
Illustrated by Gil Adams
Cover illustration by Tim Jessell

A
LITTLE APPLE
PAPERBACK

SCHOLASTIC INC.
New York Toronto London Auckland Sydney
Mexico City New Delhi Hong Kong Buenos Aires

No part of this publication may be reproduced in whole or in part, or stored in a retrieval system, or transmitted in any form or by any means, electronic, mechanical, photocopying, recording, or otherwise, without written permission of the publisher. For information regarding permission, write to Scholastic Inc., Attention: Permissions Department, 557 Broadway, New York, NY 10012.

ISBN 0-439-56040-3

Text copyright © 2003 by Robert T. Abbott
Illustrations copyright © 2003 by Scholastic Inc.

All rights reserved. Published by Scholastic Inc.
SCHOLASTIC, LITTLE APPLE, and associated logos
are trademarks and/or registered trademarks of Scholastic Inc.

12 11 10 9 8 7 6 5 4   4 5 6 7 8/0

Printed in the U.S.A.   40
First printing, October 2003

For Jennifer Bolton,
wizard, friend, and Droon's first scholar

Contents

In the Ice Caves of Krog

One

The Blizzard Wizard?

Eric Hinkle sat with his friends Julie and Neal at a table in the art room at school. He was rocking quietly in his chair. He was smiling.

"Will you sit still?" said Neal, pushing a paintbrush across a piece of paper. "I have to paint your picture. But with all your wiggling, you'll end up looking like a monkey!"

"I can't sit still," said Eric.

"At least take your gloves off," said

Julie, dipping her brush in a cup of water. "It's cold out, but you're inside now. Besides, Mrs. Michaels said we should paint. You'd better get started."

Eric looked down at his gloves and smiled again. "I can't get started. Look at this."

He glanced around the room. The other kids were busy painting or talking quietly while their teacher strolled between the tables. Making sure no one was watching, Eric took the little cup of water in front of him, lifted it high overhead, and turned it upside down.

"Eric — !" Julie shielded her picture.

But the water didn't splash out.

Thwap! A small block of ice slid out of the cup and landed in his hand.

"Whoa!" said Neal. "How did that happen?"

Eric grinned. "I touched it. And that's

not all. Since I woke up yesterday, my wizard powers have been totally nuts. I think they're getting *stronger. . . .*"

Wizard powers.

That's right. He was Eric Hinkle. Boy wizard.

As Julie and Neal leaned toward him, their eyes wide, Eric recalled how he got his powers.

He loved to remember the exact moment.

It was in Droon, of course. Where else could such a magical thing happen?

Droon was the fantastic world the three of them had discovered one day in his basement. It was a land of danger, mystery, and adventure.

Droon was also a place of amazing friends. It was there that Princess Keeah, their best friend, had saved Eric from falling into a bottomless pit.

Blam! She shot a blaze of blue wizard light.

And suddenly he was safe.

But that moment changed Eric's life forever.

Soon after, he discovered blue sparks shooting from his own fingertips. Then he began having visions of things that hadn't happened yet. And strange words popped suddenly into his head.

Magical words.

At first, he thought it had all been a weird mistake. But the great old wizard Galen told him, "I do not believe you won the powers by accident. There is a greater purpose here."

Eric knew part of that purpose, of course.

With magical powers, he could help Droon win its terrible battle against Lord Sparr.

Sparr, the sorcerer. Sparr, the ruler of the Dark Lands. Sparr, the creator of the Coiled Viper, the Red Eye of Dawn, and the Golden Wasp. Sparr the weird, Sparr the creepy, Sparr the —

"So come on already!" said Julie. "Tell us!"

"Oh, sorry." Eric took a deep breath. "Well, first of all, yesterday morning, I felt my hands getting really, really hot. A minute later, I pulled the bathroom door completely off its hinges!"

Neal gave out a low whistle. "I'm pretty sure your dad will take that out of your allowance."

"No kidding," said Eric. "Then, clearing the kitchen table last night, I broke three dishes —"

Julie winced. "I hate the sound when dishes hit the floor!"

"They didn't hit the floor," said Eric. "They hit the ceiling! That was just after I became my own personal microwave and zapped a slice of pizza to dust — right in my hand!"

Neal blinked. "Pizza? What kind of pizza —?"

"Never mind about that," said Julie. "Eric, did your parents see anything?"

He shook his head. "No. They just think I'm the king of klutziness."

Neal laughed. "Then maybe you can hang this in your palace —" He showed them his painting. Eric's head was tiny but his eyes were huge.

"Thanks a lot," Eric said with a laugh. "But here's the weirdest part of all. You know how I always shoot off blue sparks? Well . . ."

Keeping his hands under the table, Eric carefully tugged his gloves off. The instant he did, bright silver sparks blazed from his fingertips and sprayed wildly to the floor. "Cool, huh?"

"*Silver* sparks?" said Julie. "That's new."

"New and way more powerful," said Eric, tugging his gloves on and quickly painting a picture of Neal. "Even Keeah doesn't have sparks like these. I feel as if I can do anything —"

"Except maybe paint," said Neal, looking at Eric's paper. "Now *I* look like a monkey!"

Mrs. Michaels tapped her desk. "Please finish up. Put your paintings on the back table to dry."

Julie slid her watercolor kit and some paper into her pocket and went to the back of the art room. On a recent adventure in Droon, she had been scratched by a wingwolf and had gained the ability to fly and sometimes to change shape.

"I thought flying was weird," she said. "It's a piece of cake compared to Eric's new powers."

"Cake?" said Neal. "What kind of cake?"

Eric laughed as he put his painting on the table. "I have to show Keeah what I can do. I sure wish we could go to Droon right now —"

Kkkkk! A sudden crackle came over the school intercom, and a voice began to speak. "Due to the weather, school will be dismissed early. Buses will be called in five minutes!"

Eric's eyes became as huge as they were in Neal's picture. "Weather? What's going on?"

Everyone rushed to a window overlooking the courtyard. The air outside was white. Thick squashy snowflakes were swirling everywhere.

Neal gasped. "Holy cow, Eric, did you . . . ?"

"No way!" He shook his head. "I didn't do this! I *couldn't* do this. Could I?"

But his hands . . . his hands were blazing hot.

Julie frowned. "Eric, this is weird. You wanted to go home, and now we can. If your powers did this, there's only one way to find out —"

Neal's face broke into a wide grin. "To the bus, to Eric's basement, and then . . . to Droon! That is, unless Eric zaps us with a hurricane!"

"Cut it out!" said Eric as they raced out.

Ten minutes later, the three friends tumbled off the bus and ran across the yard to Eric's house.

Already the kids on the street were laughing and shouting as they dragged their sleds and saucers into the spinning snow.

"Looks like fun," said Julie. "Makes you want to have a snowball fight, doesn't it?"

Eric nodded, then saw silver sparks spring from the seams in his gloves. "We can play later. Keeah needs to see this right away. Come on!"

The friends tramped down to Eric's basement. They pushed aside three large cartons blocking a door under the stairs.

Inside was a small closet, empty except for a single lightbulb dangling from the ceiling.

They piled in. Neal closed the door behind them, and Julie pulled the light switch. *Click.*

The room went dark, but only for an instant.

Whoosh! The floor beneath them vanished, and in its place stood the top step of a staircase, shimmering in every color of the rainbow.

"I hope we never have to stop doing this," said Julie excitedly. "Droon is so awesome."

Eric couldn't help but smile. He loved it, too.

"Come on, people. To Droon!"

The three friends started down the stairs together. Passing through a layer of thick clouds, they entered a blue-black sky dotted with stars.

Icy cold air swept up around them, spinning powdery flakes of snow onto a forest below.

"It looks like Eric made it snow here, too," Neal said with a chuckle.

In the distance were the twinkling lights of a vast city of turrets and towers.

"Jaffa City," said Julie. "Keeah's hometown. These must be the Farne Woods under us. It's all so magical. I'm glad I packed my watercolors."

Barely visible through the many fir and pine trees crowded below was a faint orange glow. It was coming from a small cabin built into the trees. As the kids got closer, they saw wisps of smoke drifting up from the stone chimney.

"Keeah's cottage," said Eric. "I hope she's in there."

They all remembered the first time they had seen Keeah's house in the woods. She told them that she and her parents, King Zello and Queen Relna, had lived there when she was small.

"I hear voices from inside," said Neal.

Eric felt his neck tingle. A soft whisper flitted through the upper branches and swirled down with the flakes.

"It sounds like voices here, too," he said.

"It's the wind," said Julie. "Isn't it beautiful?"

"Let's get inside," said Neal. "Whispers give me the chills. And I'm already cold enough!"

With the snow falling more heavily around them, the three friends padded quickly to the cottage door.

Eric lifted his hand to knock.

Suddenly — *wham!* — the door came blasting open, and an enormous giant leaped out.

A giant covered entirely in fur.

A giant holding a long, sharp spear.

A giant yelling, "Ahhhhh —"

Of Harps and Happenings

"Ahhhhh!" Eric screamed, too. He jerked back into Julie and Neal as a blast of silver blew out his gloves — *zannng!* — and turned the giant's spear tip to dust.

"Oyyyy!" growled the giant loudly. "That was my muffin on there! You blew up my muffin!"

Julie gasped. "Rolf? Is that you?"

The giant bent over slowly and squinted from behind a great furry beard. "I am Rolf, official Knight of Silversnow, and you are . . . wait . . . oh, my! It's the children!"

Instantly, he scooped up the three kids and carried them inside, plopping them down before a blazing fireplace. "Everyone, lookee here!"

"Welcome!" boomed a chorus of low voices. Squeezed into the small room were two more giants, heating muffins over the fire.

"The Knights of Silversnow?" Neal yelped. "Holy cow! It's so cool to see you guys again!"

The first time the children had met them, the three legendary knights had been sleeping for centuries before Keeah woke them with a spell.

"We've been called," grumbled the knight named Lunk. "When there's trouble in Droon, everyone knows you call the best of the best!"

"Best of the best, and sleepiest, too," said the third knight, whose name was Smee. "I only woke because they said there were muffins. Well, and the monster —"

Julie blinked. "Monster? What monster?"

"Better let me tell you about that!" said a voice behind them. They turned to see a girl leap down the stairs from the room overhead. She had a gold crown twined in her long blond hair.

"Keeah!" said Eric.

"It's so good to see you all," said the princess, hugging them. Behind her on the stairs was her beautiful mother, Queen Relna, and Max, a spider troll with eight legs and fluffy orange hair.

"We're all glad you came," chirped Max. "We have a dangerous new situation in Droon!"

Eric glanced at Julie and Neal, then at his gloves. "Did somebody say *monster*?"

The queen nodded. "Galen and King Zello are on a mission to find Sparr. As you know, he discovered the magical Coiled Viper. And now he wants his two other great Powers — the Red Eye of Dawn and the Golden Wasp. "

Smee shivered. "Until that terrible Golden Wasp vanished, it had been stinging more and more people, turning them into *wraiths*!"

Lunk made a face. "I saw one once. *Eeeww!*"

The children remembered the wraiths, whispering, faceless creatures, stung by the Wasp and forced to hear only Sparr's evil voice.

"But even as my father and Galen search for Sparr," said Keeah, "there is a new problem."

All eyes turned to the princess.

"Yesterday morning, my harp began

to play by itself. Strange songs, and only for me."

She went to a shelf and pulled a bow-shaped instrument from it. Though small, the harp was full of magic. Eric remembered how its playing strangely controlled even Sparr's own Golden Wasp.

As soon as Keeah touched the strings, the harp hummed and a voice sang out. *Pling! Thrum!*

Where the water grows teeth
He wakes to new power!
All Droon fears the truth
Of his deadly bright fire!

A moment later, the harp went silent.

As much as Eric tried not to, he remembered how his sparks had burned the pizza the day before and how the ashes had crumbled right through his fingers. "What does it mean?"

"An old beast has woken up," said Keeah. "It has already attacked a village and destroyed it."

"The water grows teeth," said Neal. "Icicles are like teeth. Is the monster up where it's cold?"

Rolf beamed. "Good, Neal. Yes. The beast has awoken in northern Droon. He has many names, but we know him by his most ancient one —"

"Krog," said the queen.

The children shivered to hear the name.

"If only we could draw you a picture of Krog," chirped Max. "Then you'd be really afraid —"

"Ooh!" said Julie. "Use my paints!" She pulled her watercolor case out of her pocket.

Relna smiled. "Good idea." She dipped

Julie's brush in a cup of water and touched green paint to a piece of paper. "The face is half like a growel, half like a stumble."

"A what?" asked Eric. "I've never heard of —"

"With scales like a dracnak," grumbled Lunk, dabbing on black paint. "And quogg feet!"

"The harp sang to me of a moomflod's fiery breath," said Keeah, adding a splash of red.

Rolf, Smee, and Max added more to the painting until what emerged was a terrifying beast of great size, with fur, wings, long teeth, huge arms, thick legs, and a massive jagged tail.

"Whoa!" said Neal. "That's one ugly beast!"

"Quite right," said Smee, swallowing a whole muffin. "Only a great power will defeat Krog."

Eric suddenly felt electric. *Was this it? Was this the reason for his silver sparks?*

"A great power?" he asked. "Like this?" He pulled off his gloves, and the room shone silver.

Keeah's eyes grew huge. "Eric, this is wonderful! Even I don't have silver sparks yet!"

Relna stared at Eric as if she wanted to say something. Then she turned and swiftly pulled two giant clubs off the cabin wall. "Silver sparks mean your magic is growing, Eric. With Sparr more powerful than ever, we'll need your help. Starting with Krog."

"I'm ready," said Eric proudly. "Let's go —"

"Hush!" said Max excitedly. "Listen!"

Beyond the light tapping of flakes on the window, they heard another sound.

Sss . . . ssss!

Rolf turned. "I smell — whispers!"

Keeah and Eric ran to the window and pulled the curtains aside. One after another, dark shadows streaked across the snow toward the cabin.

"Attackers?" said Neal, stepping back with Julie and Max.

"I knew it!" said Eric. "It wasn't the wind in the branches. It was them, the faceless ones —"

An instant later — *blam!* — the cottage door burst on its hinges, and a shadow blurred into the room.

A shadow . . . without a face.

"My gosh!" cried Keeah. "It's — wraiths!"

Three

Whispers Without Words

Fwit-fwit-fwit! A trio of shadow men leaped past the first one and pounced into the room.

"This is Sparr's doing!" cried Relna, pulling the children back across the floor. "Wraiths, Sparr is your leader now, but I was once your queen. Tell me — why are you here?"

The faceless heads seemed first to stare

at her, then hiss like water striking a hot stove. *Ssss!*

"They don't talk a lot, do they?" yelled Neal.

Eric jumped forward. "Maybe they'll understand this —"

Kla-bam! Silver sparks lit up the inside of the cabin. Eric was blown to the floor, while his wild shot set the curtains on fire. "Oh, man, sorry —"

"Never mind!" Max quickly threw a pitcher of water on the bright flames, putting them out.

"Friends, get back!" cried Keeah. She sprayed a beam of blue sparks from her hands — *blam!*

It went straight for the wraiths, but the shadow men ducked low, then shot a thick fog of red sparks, scattering Keeah's light.

"Ukk!" yelled Smee, waving at the

cloud. "Smells like burnt cheese. I hate that smell!"

"Where are they?" Lunk coughed.

"One touched me!" shouted Neal, tumbling to the floor and trying to scramble away.

"I'll help you!" Julie dashed across the room, grabbed Neal, and flew straight up to the ceiling. "Stay away from my friends, you icky wraiths!"

Sssss! More shadow creatures blurred into the room, pointed at Keeah, then lunged at her.

"Oh, no you don't!" Queen Relna sent a second beam of blue sparks at the wraiths, scattering them long enough for her to pull Keeah into a corner. "They're after you. This way, come —"

"Fellows, form a line!" cried Rolf, chomping one last muffin. "Knights of Silversnow, charge!"

The warriors leaped up, shoulder to furry shoulder, and pushed the wraiths to the door.

"Friends, come on!" said Keeah. She let loose a final spray of sparks, then grabbed the children and Max and followed her mother.

Relna darted into the tiny back room. *Errk!* She pulled on a creaky floorboard. Curving away under the cottage was a dark tunnel.

"The wraiths are on some new mission from Sparr," she said. "Keeah, you must go. Take your harp. It may help you stop Krog. Hurry!"

Keeah's eyes showed fear, but she nodded sharply, tightened her harp on her shoulder, kissed her mother, and dropped into the hole.

Julie, Neal, and Max followed next.

Then Eric dropped his legs into the hole.

"Eric, wait," said the queen. "The wraiths are after Keeah, just as the beast is after our villages. Stop Krog, and keep Keeah safe!"

C-c-crashhhhh! The shattering of glass made Relna turn. "Eric, I'm depending on you!"

He gulped. "I'll do my best!"

Sliding into the hole, he pulled the board back into place. The smell of earth surrounded him.

My best? I can't even control my sparks!

"Eric, are you there?" Keeah asked from the darkness ahead.

"Coming," he said, crawling his way to her.

"Stop Krog? Keep Keeah safe?" he muttered, looking once more at his hands. "I wish!"

As the small band squirmed deeper into

the ground, the sounds of fighting grew quieter. Finally, the tunnel ended in a round wooden wall.

"I think we've come out in a tree," chirped Max. "Come along, my friends."

Pop! The door swung open to the outside.

But as warm as the cabin had been, the night air was freezing. The cold seemed to slap their faces harshly as they crawled from the tree.

Keeah turned back. Two wraiths were tumbling out of the cottage window. "I should stay to help my mother and the knights."

Relna's words still in his mind, Eric pulled Keeah deeper into the woods. "Your mom will be okay. She's superpowerful. Right now she wants us to find Krog. And help Droon —"

"Help the queen, help Droon?" boomed a voice. "How about helping me?"

The kids turned to see the top half of old Rolf poking up through the tree hole, his bottom half still stuck in the tunnel. "Just a little tug, please?"

Laughing, Neal and Julie grabbed one arm, while Keeah, Eric, and Max pulled the other.

"Thankee!" Rolf boomed as he plopped free. "Now, our queen and my knights are more than a match for wraiths," he said. "Our job is to stop Krog and shut down his dreaded ice caves —"

"Uh . . . *ice* caves?" asked Neal, stepping back. "But my toes are frozen already!"

Max burst out with laughter. "The beast lives in the place that gave winter its name! I will weave us all some warm clothes." With a swift blur, the spider troll spun four pairs of thick silken boots and fuzzy coats to match.

"Thank you, Max," said Keeah. She

looked one last time at the cottage, then turned to her friends. "Okay, then, everyone. If my mother wants us to find Krog, then we'll find Krog."

"And stop him," said Julie.

"I'm ready," said Neal. "Where is this beast?"

"In the North!" Rolf boomed. He didn't move.

Everyone looked at him.

He still didn't move.

Eric frowned. "But North is a big place."

"North!" The Knight of Silversnow put a finger in his mouth, licked it, then stuck it triumphantly in the air. "North . . . is . . . it's . . . North is . . . well . . . it should be . . . it's near . . ."

"It's there," grumbled Max, pointing over his left shoulder. "North is that way."

"Of course!" said Rolf, turning entirely around and hitching his shield on his back.

"To the ice caves of Krog, everyone, for an old-fashioned beastie quest! Under the cover of night, too!"

Max made a face. "It's always night in the North, you know. Come on. Bundle up tight."

He followed Rolf across the first of many snowdrifts leading north.

The children shared a look.

Keeah slung her harp on her shoulder and sighed. "Oy."

Eric grinned. "That's pretty much what I was going to say."

With no more words, the children ran to catch up with Rolf and together bent to the fierce weather ahead.

To find Krog in the cold, dark night.

The very cold and very dark night.

Four

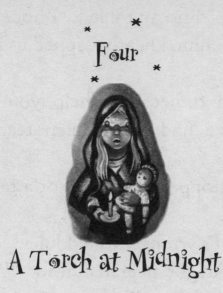

A Torch at Midnight

One hour . . . Two hours . . . Rolf led the small band into the North. Whatever lights they saw soon twinkled away to nothing, while the wind blew snow deeper and deeper around them.

"I thought the blizzard at home was bad," said Neal, tightening his coat. "This is way worse!"

"Krog will be worse still," said Max.

"Krog," Eric mumbled. "I hope we're a match for him. I nearly zapped us all in the cabin."

Keeah turned. "I'll help you practice before we find him. Galen teaches me how —"

Rolf stopped at the top of a tall snowbank.

"What's wrong?" asked Julie.

The knight peered ahead. "Well, it's that teeny-weeny little path. I saw it just a minute ago. . . ."

"Wait!" Max thrust up a furry hand and went still. He sniffed the air. "That smell . . ."

"Do you smell burnt cheese again?" asked Keeah, whirling around. "Is it wraiths?"

Julie shook her head. "No, smoke." She pointed to where the snow was clearing. "There . . ."

Eric shuddered to see it.

Ahead of them, plumes of black smoke rose from a small village. Or what had once been a village. House after house was now no more than a smoking, charred pile of blackened lumber.

"What did the harp sing about Krog?" said Neal. "His deadly bright fire? He sure must have used it here."

As they made their way into the village, Eric looked up. Over the noise of the whirling snow, another sound seemed to move in the air.

Was it whispers? Were wraiths following them? Or was it something else?

"I see a light," gasped Julie. "Hide!"

The friends scurried behind a broken fireplace as a dim orange flame jerked toward them. It dipped and halted, then came forward again.

"Wraiths don't advertise like that,"

whispered Keeah. "Come on, but let's be careful."

They crept along a snowy street, then stopped.

Out of the distance came a young girl holding a candle. Her face was dark with soot. Draped over her shoulders was a tattered black shawl.

She stopped, too. "Please, don't hurt me."

Neal shook his head. "We're after Krog."

"Who are you?" asked Julie.

"My name is Motli," said the little girl.

"Did you see the monster?" asked Eric. "Where did everyone go? Where did Krog go?"

The girl looked down. "Krog came and everyone ran away, except one. . . ." She stopped.

"One?" grunted Rolf. "One who?"

"The prince," she said. "The Prince of Stars."

Max frowned. "Prince of Stars? Well, I've been around for a while, and I've never heard of him."

"Oh, he was mysterious," said Motli. "And magical. His eyes glowed as green as emeralds. He fought Krog all the way to the ice caves."

"The ice caves!" snorted Rolf. "We can't seem to find them —"

As if in response — *ploing!* — the harp suddenly struck a note and started singing.

Find the wild street of fish.
Step upon the floating dish!

Motli's eyes widened. "Your harp is magical!"

Keeah nodded. "It is. But often it doesn't make any sense. Like now, for instance. Street of fish?"

Suddenly, Neal exploded. "I'm a genius!"

Julie laughed. "That's a stretch."

"Okay, so I'm not a genius," said Neal. "But I think I understand part of the song. A street is where people go, right? Where do fish go? In water. In a river!"

Motli laughed brightly. "There is a river not far from here. Come. I will show it to you."

Neal beamed as he rushed after the girl. "You see? I am a genius. We got a river!"

As everyone jumped after her, Eric paused and listened to the snow spinning around him. Then he looked at the sparks beaming from his fingertips. "There's something too easy about this," he murmured. "A few minutes ago, we were lost in the blizzard. Suddenly, we know the way. It's almost —"

"Magical?" said Keeah, slowing to a stop.

Eric turned to her. "Yeah. And I keep

hearing something, but I don't know what it is."

"Me, too," she said. "But it's not wraiths. Let's get to the others and be on our guard."

Splash! Splurshhh! Motli led them to the banks of a heaving, wild river. Waves crashed up and down in the icy black water.

Rolf put his hands on his hips. "Humf! Genius or no, Neal, that's too rough to cross."

"Wide, too," said Neal. "The harp said wild street, but that's more like a wild highway!"

"Maybe there's another way?" asked Julie.

"The prince used a raft to cross when he first came to the village," said Motli. "Here it is."

She pulled aside some weeds where a crisscross of wooden planks lay hidden. The moment Motli untied the raft —

shoosh! — the roaring water went suddenly calm, making a glassy path across the river from the bank.

"Awesome!" whispered Julie. "I guess the Prince of Stars knew about magic, all right."

Keeah gave Eric a look as, one by one, the small group piled onto the raft, and it began to glide calmly across the water.

"Ha!" said Rolf. "Good thing the words of the harp are telling us how to find Krog. I'd get us lost. But no fear, we'll soon face the beast."

Eric nodded. "Soon. Maybe too soon."

As the raft moved over the river, Keeah turned to him. "Galen once told me that real power is knowing when to use it and when not to use it."

Neal chuckled. "Eric isn't using it too well."

"Words control your magic, Eric," said Keeah. Then she whispered in his ear and pointed across the water.

He raised his hands. *"Seepo-ta-la-moo!"*

Zannng! A blast of silver air burst from his fingertips in a bright arc of light. It hung in the sky.

Eric's heart leaped. "This is so amazing. It did what I wanted it to. These sparks light up everything!"

"Even *that,*" said Max. "Look —"

Under the blaze of Eric's beam, they all saw a circle of land floating in the middle of the river. On it stood a mountain twisting to the sky.

"An island!" said Neal. "That's what the harp was singing about. *Step upon the floating dish.* Krog is there!"

Even as the children cheered, Eric's eyes were drawn back to the shore. Under the fading light of his sparks, he saw a branch stir. Snow spun suddenly. A soft hissing drifted across the water.

"Guys, I think I have some bad news," he murmured. "Look at the riverbank. The wraiths followed us. Neal, get us to the island right away —"

"Me?" said Neal, turning. "I'm not steering this thing. I thought Rolf was steering!"

"Me?" boomed the knight. "But isn't Motli?"

"*No one's* controlling this thing!" cried Julie.

Even as the raft sped on, a dozen wraiths dived from the bank and into the river. In seconds, they grasped at the side of the raft.

Eric jumped up. "Keeah, I'll protect us — oh!"

He never had a chance to use his sparks.

K-k-krash! The raft knocked up against the island's shore. In seconds, the river grew wild once more, the wraiths went hissing back into the water, and the kids toppled into one another.

"Help!" shrieked Motli, tumbling over.

Instantly, the icy water swallowed the girl.

"I'll save her!" cried Max, scrambling up.

"But, Max!" yelled Keeah. "Max!"

Splash! The icy water swallowed him, too.

Five

The Iceman Comes . . . and Goes

Even as Rolf and the children jumped to shore, the wild black waves pulled Max and Motli swiftly down the river.

Blam! Keeah's sparks sent the wraiths back farther. "Eric, use the words —"

"*Seepo-ta-la-moo!*" he cried out.

Zannng! His sparks exploded high, casting a light over the far bank. The wraiths were gathering there for another charge at the kids.

"They're coming back for more," said Julie.

Rolf jumped. "But there, everyone . . . look!"

From the waves, as if shot from below — *sploosh!* — Motli burst up and out, her black shawl billowing with air as if she had wings.

"My gosh!" said Keeah. "She's flying!"

"M-m-m-me, to-o-o-o!" Max was cling-ing to Motli's back as she soared higher and higher.

Eric stared, astonished. "There *is* magic here."

Suddenly, Motli dived, scattering the wraiths back into the dark night.

"Children, go!" cried Max as they flew up again. "S-s-stop . . . K-K-Krog! I'll be okay-y-y. I think-k-k!"

"Max!" said Keeah. "Oh, Max —"

As Eric's silver sparks faded over the wild water, the strange little girl, the spider troll, and the wraiths themselves vanished into the snowstorm. Moments later, the winter night surrounded the children again.

Julie stared at the sky. "That was so amazing."

"One thing I know," said Rolf, scanning the spot where their friends had vanished. "Max will return. He must! Who else would poke fun at me?"

As they all stood silently on the island's shore, Eric recalled the spider troll's words.

Stop Krog.

They were the same words Relna had said to him. He turned to his friends. "Come on, people. Our group is smaller, but we have to go on."

Without looking back, Eric headed up

the steep slope of the island's icy mountain, the others following.

With every step, the wind grew more fierce, and the path snaked and looped around the mountain, seeming to double back on itself.

"Have we done this before?" asked Julie, trudging after Rolf. "These drifts seem familiar."

The old knight slowed and licked his finger.

Neal stopped short. "No more!" he snapped. "Give me palmtrees, give me beach chairs, give me french fries. I've had it with the cold and snow and ice and being lost —"

Pling-g-g-g!

Everyone hushed.

"The harp!" gasped Keeah. She pulled the magical instrument around. The wind seemed to brush the strings, and it began to play.

The ribbon ties, the ribbon breaks.
Pass the test of the stomachaches!

Julie frowned. "What does that mean?"

"I'm too cold to think," grumbled Neal.

Eric peered ahead. "I'm not the best at figuring out songs, but I think it means *that!*"

Out of the whirling snow before them, they could see that the path continued for a while up the mountain.

Then it didn't.

Just visible in the snow ahead was a deep chasm, cut into the earth. Drooping across the chasm, wide enough for only one person, was a creaking bridge of ice, barely two inches thick.

Keeah gulped. "The harp sang about ribbons. Ribbons are for presents. This is no present."

"Yeah," said Neal, "but a ribbon's any kind of skinny strip. Like a ribbon of ice. Like a bridge."

Julie made a face. "Neal, you're good at solving riddles. Too bad you don't have good news."

Eric looked up. He felt a tingle down his neck.

"You're all good at this," grumbled Rolf. "You remind me of Galen when he was young. But if I step on that bridge, I'll crack it in two!"

Keeah nodded. "We already lost Max. We're not going on without you. Maybe there's another way across the chasm."

But the moment they turned — *whoomf!* — snow exploded from the ground, and a large, shaggy warrior, covered with white fur and long icicles, lurched up from the earth.

"Groooo!" the creature growled, showing white fangs as long as pencils. "No one passes this way unless they answer my riddles!"

"Holy cow!" gasped Eric. "Who are you?"

"I am the iceman!" the creature replied, picking up a giant rock of ice in his clawed hands.

"You look more like a snowman," said Julie.

"Yeah, why don't you melt?" snapped Neal.

The iceman glared angrily at Neal. "For that, *you* must answer my riddles!"

Neal stepped back into Eric. "Me?"

"You!" said the iceman. "First, what

happens when you cross a flimple with a plabb?"

"A what with a who?" asked Eric.

Keeah jumped. She used her magic to speak silently to Neal.

"Um . . . you get a moople?" said Neal.

"Correct!" shouted the iceman, shaking his fur. "Second, what happens when you kleep?"

Rolf laughed. He whispered in Neal's ear.

Neal grinned. "You get a very sore bungle!"

"*Groooo!* Correct! And now for the last —"

"This isn't fair!" said Neal. "Ask something regular. Something from the Upper World."

Julie made a face. "Neal —"

The iceman howled. "Regular? Okay.

What's five hundred and sixteen divided by forty-three?"

Everyone looked at Neal.

"Math?" He gulped. "What am I, a genius?"

Eric grumbled. "Neal, you said you were —"

"No answer? Wrong!" The iceman lifted his giant rock and shook his fur.

"Back, everyone!" yelled Rolf. "This is my moment!" In one quick movement, he herded the kids to the ice bridge. Then he slid them one by one to the far side as if they were bowling balls.

"Stay put over there!" he said. "I promised the queen you wouldn't get hurt — and you won't! Save your fancy powers for Krog!"

Then he turned. "Okay, shaggy! Here I come!"

But the iceman was ready for him.

Whoom! — It hurled its giant boulder fast.

"Rolf!" Keeah cried.

Rolf threw up his shield, but the rock struck it with a tremendous crash, knocking him back.

Groaning, the knight staggered, rolled his eyes, then slumped to his knees.

On the bridge.

The children gasped. "Rolffff — get off —!"

The bridge creaked and swayed and wobbled.

The iceman leaped at Rolf in a flash. But together they were too heavy for the ice.

K-k-r-r-e-e-k-k! The bridge shattered into a hundred pieces and fell into the chasm below.

"*Grooooo?*" howled the iceman.

He went down first.

"Oy!" snorted Rolf.

He fell, too.

"Ooof! Ugh! Oyyyyy! *Grooo!*"

The two giants bounced noisily every inch of the way to the snow-filled dark depths below.

Palace of Doughnuts

"Rollllfffff!" Julie cried at the top of her lungs.

"Stop-p-p . . . K-K-Krog!" came the response.

The words rang up from the chasm, echoing over and over again. Then there was nothing.

"The ribbon breaks," said Julie, looking at the broken bridge. "Just like the harp sang. Rolf fought the beast for us and now he's gone."

"Just like Max," said Keeah.

Eric half expected the iceman to fly Rolf up from the depths, but there was only silence.

"I can't believe it," he murmured.

"Then you won't believe *that,* either," said Neal.

Everyone looked up.

On the mountain's peak just above them were the walls and towers of a giant castle made of ice and snow. Set high in the walls were windows flickering with warm orange light.

"Where did that come from?" asked Keeah.

"I don't know, but it's beautiful," said Julie. Her eyes wide in disbelief, she took out her watercolors. Dabbing her brush in the snow, she quickly began painting a picture.

"This is so weird," said Eric. "We're supposed to find the dreaded ice caves of Krog. Instead we see a nice warm palace sitting on a mountain on an island in the middle of a snowstorm?"

Neal laughed. "And you're complaining? If it's warm in there, we're going in. Come on!"

Together, the small band climbed the last few steps to the castle. Neal pushed open the doors.

Whoosh! Warm air flooded over the children.

"Welcome!" shouted a high voice. "Come in!"

The children turned to see a short, squat man tramping down a long hall toward them. He wore a bright red cape and giant red boots.

"So glad you could come!" said the man.

Keeah took a step. "We're looking for —"

"Krog, Krog, yes, I know," said the little man, whipping his cape around him. "Beast of beasts. He fought the Prince of Stars —"

"You know about the prince?" asked Eric.

"Wonderful man. Eyes as green as emeralds!"

That's what Motli said, Eric said to himself. *What's going on here? More. . . magic?*

"Now come," said the man. "First you must eat, then it's off to find Krog! Look him in the eyes and — *ka-pow!*"

He waddled down the hall. "Come! Food!"

The kids looked at one another, even as they followed the little man. Entering a large room, Neal stopped short, then jumped.

"Food?" he cried. "Look at all the

doughnuts!" He jumped to a table heaped high with platters. "I've been thinking about doughnuts all day!"

"You do that every day," said Julie. "But I don't see any doughnuts. All I see is corn chips, which is okay by me." She popped a handful of chips into her mouth. *Crunchhh!*

Eric scanned the table. He saw nothing but plates of apple pie. "Hey, what's going on —"

"Droon potato soup!" said Keeah, lifting a big bowl to her lips. "I am so hungry . . . *mmm* . . . ."

Even as he slid a slice of pie into his mouth and munched, Eric looked around. "Did you see where the man went? This is kind of strange."

"Nothing's strange about me and doughnuts," said Neal. "Don't you get it?

We're seeing our favorite foods. Jelly-filled? Jelly is good."

"Good?" said Julie, putting down the chips. "Actually, I'm not sure I feel so goo . . . ooo . . . oood . . . oh!" She flopped onto the table — *plunk!* — and began to snore.

Keeah looked over. "Julie?"

Eric felt his ears beginning to buzz. He felt hot. "I think something's wrong —"

"It's a trick," said Keeah suddenly. "The food . . . the test of the . . . stomach-aches . . ."

"What? Keeah —"

The princess slumped to a chair, then rolled to the floor, fast asleep, her harp toppling. *Ploing!*

Before you tumble off to sleep,
The crumbs from heaven's table sweep!

Eric slid into a chair, feeling heavy. "Sleep? No . . . Neal . . . the food is making us . . . sleep!"

Neal was on his knees. "Too much . . . jelly."

Eric tried to reach him. "Crumbs from heaven's table . . . Neal . . . what do the words mean?"

His friend rolled to the floor. "Heaven's table? Maybe . . . the sky? Crumbs . . . snowflakes —"

Neal's head hit the floor. He was asleep.

There was a sudden sound of flapping. Looking up, Eric saw that the ceiling was a dome of ice. Amid the snow whirling over it, he thought he spied a bird circling in the flakes.

Snowflakes, he thought. *Like crumbs from the sky . . . from heaven's table . . .*

That's when he knew.

They needed snow.

Even as he closed his eyes, Eric aimed his fingers up at the icy dome. As if someone whispered to him, words came flooding to his lips. They sounded silly, but he said them anyway.

"Chengo . . . la . . . moop!"

Zzzzang! A silver beam of light left his fingers and shot like an arrow to the dome.

Whooooomf! The ceiling melted away.

His strength gone, Eric fell to the floor as tiny flakes of snow spilled into the room, swirling and whirling in the air all the way down to the four children.

The snow melted to cold water on their faces.

Eric felt himself falling and falling. Everything was going dark around him.

Suddenly, a voice was shouting in his ear.

"Up you go! Come on! Hurry!

The next thing he knew, his eyes were opening and Keeah was pulling him up from the floor.

"Eric, you did it!" she cried. "You saved us. The snow woke us up. Now, come on. The palace is disappearing!"

"What?" Eric shook his head clear. His friends were all scrambling up, and on every side of them the huge palace of ice was melting away.

Tsss! A flake of snow landed on the table of food. *Tsss!* The table dissolved to nothing. *Tsss!* Snow struck the floor. *Tsss!* The icy floor melted.

Tsss! Tsss! Tsss! In seconds, the walls, the doors, the great ice palace itself were nothing more than damp splotches on the mountaintop.

"Where did my doughnuts go?" asked Neal.

"Where did it *all* go?" asked Julie.

The four friends were outside again.

Everything had vanished around them, leaving only the snow and the night and the cold.

"We were tricked," said Keeah. "The palace was enchanted. It was all a magic spell, a spell that has ended."

"But this is real," said Eric. "Look."

Where the palace had been now stood a tall open arch cut deep into the mountain's peak.

"The ice caves," said Eric, fully awake now. "We found the ice caves of Krog —"

As if in response, a terrible roar sounded from within. *Rooaaaw-ooaaw!*

Neal turned. "Do we really have to go in?"

Eric glanced at Keeah. She nodded.

"Neal," he said, "we have to go in."

The beast roared again, shaking the earth.

Rooaaarrrr!

Slowly, the four friends stepped into the ice caves of the beast.

Seven

Lots of Loot

Darkness loomed ahead. Jagged icicles hung like a fringe of swords over their heads as the children entered the cave.

"Nice decoration," said Neal, glancing at the icy spikes. "I just hope we don't get the point!"

The walls were rounded on either side of them, forming a tunnel. Five steps in, it dipped and wormed its way deep into the mountain.

"It's a long way down," said Julie, peering into the tunnel. "And it looks even colder in there."

Keeah gulped, then managed a smile. "At least the four of us are all together."

Eric smiled, too. He recalled Relna's words. *Keep Keeah safe.* He was glad she was there. He was glad all his friends were there.

Then he stopped smiling. Relna's other words came to him again. *Stop Krog.*

He couldn't help feeling that they had been brought to the ice caves by magic. The magic of the harp. The magic of the castle.

Would the caves turn out to be some kind of test, like the castle seemed to be?

Were his powers ready for Krog?

"Come on," said Keeah. "We've come a long way for the beast. He's in here. Let's find him."

The princess lowered herself into the tunnel, and the others followed, finding rough footholds and bumpy rocks to help them climb down.

"I wonder if Sparr knows about this place," said Julie as they descended. "It's dark enough and cold enough."

Neal snorted. "And nasty enough. Like him."

Thump. Keeah jumped down, landing on the ice at the bottom. "I see fire ahead."

Lured by a growing light at the far end of the tunnel, the group crept on together. But as the tunnel widened into a cave, they stopped short.

The light Keeah had seen wasn't from a fire.

It came from the cold shine of frozen metal.

Neal gasped. "Holy cow . . . *gold!*"

Heaps of goblets, piles of swords,

stacks of chests, mounds of armor, spears, and crowns together formed a golden mountain in the ice cave.

"I have to paint this," said Julie. "After the creepy picture of Krog, I can finally paint something beautiful." Warming some ice with her hands, she dipped her brush in the water and quickly painted the vast treasure cave.

Krog roared again, closer this time.

"We should probably . . ." Keeah paused. "We should find some . . . weapons." From among the piles of treasure she pulled out a long silk rope. "Maybe we can tie him up."

"How about this?" asked Julie, spotting a small wooden club. "It reminds me of Rolf. Maybe I can scare Krog with it."

A deep green pouch nearby caught Eric's eye. It wasn't much of a weapon, he thought, but the color made him recall what had been said about the mysterious Prince of Stars.

That his eyes were the color of emeralds.

Neal sniffed the small pouch. "It's filled with water, you know. But that's okay. I'll be thirsty after I defeat Krog with my amazing — torch!" He held a black cone high in the air. Leaping from the end of it was a vibrant yellow flame.

Then, while the treasure shone more brightly in the torch's glow, Keeah gasped. "Rolf's shield!" She ran right to a giant shield with a snowflake design on it. "Krog has him —"

Thwump-ump! A thunderous rumble came from the side caves. Ice cracked in the distance.

Neal gasped. "It's h-h-h-him! It's Krog! And he knows we're here messing with his stuff!"

"He does now, Mr. Noisy!" said Julie, dragging Neal behind a rock. "Here he comes!"

Thwump! Suddenly, the cave itself quaked, and in the light of the treasure and the flames of Neal's torch, the kids saw a monster with wings, a thick, jagged tail, and a massive body covered with long fur, scales, and knobby skin.

"Krog," said Julie softly.

Neal staggered back. "And that painting of him isn't *half* as scary as the real guy himself!"

The beast stared at the children one by one.

"He reminds me of . . . Sparr," whispered Eric.

Keeah took a breath, then said loudly, "We've come to stop you, Krog. And we will —"

Bellowing a laugh, the beast uncoiled

his huge length of tail and snapped its spiky end like a whip. *Thwapp-apppp!*

Before anyone could move, Neal's torch was pulled from his hand and dashed to the ground, and he himself was thrown to the wall in a heap.

"Everyone, charge now!" said Keeah. She looped her rope and threw it at Krog lasso-style.

Krog swung his head and sneezed out a fire.

Wumpf! Its bright flame charred the loop of Keeah's rope and danced swiftly back at her.

"Keeah!" Eric cried, stumbling over the rocks to her, but Krog's long spiked tail scraped along the treasure, hurling goblets and crowns at him.

"Don't you hurt my friends!" Julie shouted. She flew across the cave, swinging her club high.

Slorpppp! Krog unraveled his tongue. Ripping Julie's club from her hand, he pulled it right into his gaping jaws. *Crunch!*

"That's rude!" Julie fell dazed to the floor.

Eric dodged the flying treasure and charged. Words were coming to him, forming in his mind. He raised his hands, even as the beast turned.

"Salba-maa —"

"Eric, blast Krog!" called Neal. "Do it!"

Wham! Krog's clawed fist punched the cave wall hard. Giant chunks of ice crashed down from the ceiling.

"Eric!" cried Keeah. "Get back!"

As hard as he tried, Eric didn't have time to run. Great pieces of ice tumbled at him, and he slid down into a dark side tunnel. "Keeah!"

Foooom-oom! Eric fell, covering his face as he went down. The ceiling thundered again and again with deafening roars. Luckily, Eric landed under a ledge, protecting him from the crash of tumbling rocks.

Finally, the noise stopped, and there was silence. Slowly, Eric lifted his head. He shook the ice and rocks off him and opened his eyes.

The heavy head of the beast turned to him.

Even in the dim light, Eric saw that he was in another cave. His friends were nowhere around.

Then he saw something else.

There was no way out.

Eight

I Only Have Ice for You

Eric stood up, balancing on the broken stones, keeping his eyes fixed on Krog.

The beast breathed slowly, looking at him.

Krog was huge. Powerful. To Eric, he seemed like the most evil monster ever.

Like Sparr, almost.

Krog had destroyed villages. He had stolen treasure. He had battled the Prince of Stars. He had Rolf's shield. Maybe he had Rolf himself.

As Eric watched him, Krog's jaws opened wide. They dripped a thick, oozy liquid.

Then the beast's mind seemed to speak right to Eric's. *Are y-y-ou h-here to d-d-defeat me, boy?*

Eric staggered back. "So! You can talk?"

To y-y-you.

"That's a pretty good wizard trick!"

I have t-t-two weaknesses-s-s.

Eric glanced around. There was no way out, but there was something. . . .

Nearby, a bridge of ice ran across the cave. It was piled with huge boulders. If Eric could get onto the bridge and lure Krog to it, he'd be higher than the beast. He just might have a chance.

"Weaknesses, huh?"

The beast took a thundering step.

T-t-two. And-d-d they're v-v-very smal-l-l!

Eric thought back. Had he shown Krog his power? His silver light? No. He hadn't shown it.

The beast again moved toward him, but even in the freezing lair of the monster, Eric felt the great magic in his hands.

He was a wizard. He had silver power. Keeah had helped him to use it. And words were starting to come to him. But he needed to surprise Krog. To catch him off guard. To trick him.

He'd make Krog think he was just a kid.

Eric felt a smile move across his lips.

That's it, he thought, *just a kid.*

"You've got weaknesses, all right," he called. "How about these — you're green and dumb!"

Eric shot across the cave and climbed

onto the bridge. He scrambled out to the big boulders.

D-do you like to w-w-walk tight-t-t-ropes?

Krog sent a flame at the bridge, melting it.

"Okay," said Eric. "This is *my* big moment!"

He whipped his pouch around and emptied it. In the frigid air — *slurrk!* — the water froze into an icicle. Just as another flame shot at the bridge, Eric wedged the icicle under a huge rock.

"Say *cheese!*" Eric pushed down hard on the icicle.

The boulder wobbled, then fell. Before Krog could move — *bloink!* — the rock fell on the tip of his snout. The beast stumbled for an instant.

Holding his breath, Eric jumped, landing on Krog's head. He aimed his fingers,

prepared to send a stream of silver light at Krog. It would stop him for good. Eric stared at the beast's face.

"Time's up, Krog!" he cried.

The beast's eyes were green.

"I'll stop you!" Sparks shot off Eric's fingers.

Eyes as green as emeralds.

"What — ?" Eric paused for an instant.

Zzz . . . His sparks fizzled to nothing.

Krog searched Eric's face, but didn't move.

"No . . . no . . ." Eric slid to the floor, staggering on his feet next to the beast. "Your eyes . . . your two weaknesses . . . I can't believe it. . . ."

Krog kept staring, as if he were reading Eric's mind. Eric stared back until, finally, he spoke.

"You're him. You're . . . the Prince of Stars!"

As if the words themselves were filled with magic, the monstrous beast began to change.

His wings collapsed away on the icy floor, and the fur and scales that draped Krog's body shrank into a cloak as blue-black as the sky itself. And a helmet, bronze and battered, formed over the head, shielding the nose and cheeks . . . of a man.

Krog the beast was gone.

In his place was a man, tall and cloaked and booted, with eyes as green as emeralds.

Quietly, he spoke. "You saved my life."

Eric blinked. "You are the Prince of Stars. . . ."

"Some call me that, yes."

"But . . . how?" Eric said. "Who are you?"

The man turned to the far side of the cave. When he moved, sparks — like tiny stars — scattered around him, making a sound like fingers brushing the strings of a harp.

"In truth, I do not know," he said. "Long ago, I was in a battle and was hurt. Afterward, I had no memory of who I was. I have wandered Droon in secret, searching for an answer."

"But what about . . . Krog?" asked Eric.

The man smiled. "Krog is — was — an ancient, mysterious, and cursed beast. Yesterday, I happened on his path and met him in battle. I struck him down, but I was wounded."

He touched his arm as he spoke.

"Within hours, I began to change into him. That is when I discovered the real curse. Destroy Krog and you become the monster yourself. . . ."

Eric heard voices yelling. "My friends."

The prince approached the cave wall.

"If you and your friends hadn't come when you did, I would have become the beast in my heart. After that, if you had used your powers, Krog wouldn't have fallen, but I would have. You saved me."

Eric felt breathless. "Someone told me that real power is knowing when to use it and when not to use it. I guess we did okay?"

For the first time, the prince laughed. It was a chiming laugh, like a harp strummed joyfully.

His hand touched the wall.

Vrrrt! The ice parted onto the treasure cave.

"Eric!" cried Keeah. Everyone rushed to him.

He laughed as he introduced the prince, who bowed, spraying more stars around him.

"Thank you all for saving me," said the

prince. Then he pointed toward the trea-sure. "Now, look there to see your friends —"

"Oyyyy!" boomed a voice. "Blast some Kroggy flame on these cold muffins, will you?"

The kids turned. Tramping across the golden heaps were two figures.

"Rolf!" yelled Neal. "And Max, too!"

The Knight of Silversnow and the spi-der troll hurried over and hugged their friends.

"The iceman dumped me here with Max and some muffins," snorted Rolf. "Good muffins!"

"Motli flew me here safe and sound," Max chirped. "But how did you ever find the caves?"

"As for that!" The prince whistled. Sud-denly, the caves resounded with the sound of flapping.

"Wings?" said Eric. "What is this? I've heard the sound of wings all day!"

In an instant, three tattered crows, with red, white, and black feathers, swept into the treasure room and perched on the prince's shoulders.

"Meet Otli, Jotli, and Motli," said the prince. "Birds who like to change shape —"

"And help a friend!" chirped the black crow.

Eric gasped. "I knew it! The second we were lost, someone pointed us in the right direction."

Keeah laughed. "Motli was there to show us the river." She pointed at the black crow.

It bowed to them. "Glad to be of service!"

"And the iceman only attacked when we decided not to cross the bridge," said Julie.

Otli, the white bird, bowed. *"Grooo!"*

Neal nodded. "And that little guy who tried to make us sleep — I bet he was testing us to see if we would keep going!"

"A test you nearly failed," said Jotli, fluffing its red feathers.

"We were guided from the beginning," said Julie. "We had all those crazy harp riddles."

The prince laughed again. "I hoped that if you understood the riddles and passed the test, you would solve Krog's mystery. Which you did —"

CRACKKKK!

The ice caves thundered, and instantly, the air filled with the sounds of hissing and spitting.

"Evil creatures of the Wasp!" cried Max.

Keeah gasped. "Wraiths! They followed us!"

"Behind me!" said the prince.

But the shadow creatures were ruthless and swift. They dived at Keeah, pushed her down, and wrenched the magic harp from her. *Sssss! Sss!*

"What?" cried the prince. "Those words —"

Eric shot his sparks back at the wraiths — *zannng!* — but it was too late. The wraiths were gone as quickly as they had come, vanishing away in the cold darkness.

Eric rushed to help Keeah up. "It was the harp that Sparr's men wanted, not you —"

"We shall get the harp back!" said the prince, his green eyes flashing. "Come. I must show you something. Children, Max, Rolf — follow me!"

Nine

Racing the Wraiths

The Prince of Stars ran to the center of the treasure cave. "Yesterday, after the fight, I saw something among the treasure. It's gone now."

Julie took out the picture she had painted of the golden treasure. "Then it wouldn't be here."

The prince grinned. "Not anymore, but wait."

He ran his hand over the picture and

whispered strange words. Instantly, what had been a simple watercolor began to move like a movie.

"Now, that's very cool!" said Neal.

"This is yesterday," said the prince. "There!"

The picture moved slowly over piles and piles of golden things when suddenly, a necklace burst into the air, then a goblet, then a sword.

Finally, a curved tail popped out of the heap.

Something was working its way from the pile.

"What is it?" asked Eric, peering closer.

Then Keeah gasped. "The tail . . . the wings . . . it's the . . . Wasp! It's the Golden Wasp —"

"Sparr's second great Power!" chittered Max.

"It's bigger than it was," said Julie. "Lots!"

In the picture, the Wasp lifted over the treasure. Even as they watched, the creature grew larger. Its wings blurred swiftly, then it changed direction and flew up and out of the caves.

The watercolor went still once more.

"So! After months," said Rolf, "this is where the Wasp had vanished to, the terrible thing."

Keeah breathed deeply. "Krog must have stolen the Wasp and brought it here. But it came alive and will find its way back to Sparr. The wraiths stole my harp because it can control the Wasp. And now Sparr will have both!"

The prince shook his head. "Listen. What remains of the beast in me heard the wraiths hissing about Sparr. They will meet in Jaffa City —"

Keeah gasped. "My mother —"

"Shall be safe!" said the prince. He

pointed to a golden sled half hidden in the clutter. "Come help me. This will take us to Jaffa City!"

Rolf and Max, together with the kids, helped drag out the sled. One by one, they piled in.

"Everyone ready?" asked Eric.

The birds on the prince's shoulder crowed.

"Good-bye, ice caves!" said the prince.

"Let's go!" said Keeah.

With a sprinkle of stars, the prince took the controls, and — *foom-foom-foom!* — the sled shot up through the tunnels and out into the snow. Then, as if it were flying, the sled barreled down the mountain, splashed across the river, and roared over the snowbanks of the north.

As the sky began to lighten toward dawn, the small band spied a mass of towers and domes.

"Jaffa City!" cried Keeah. "Home."

Home, thought Eric. *But a home under attack*.

The real Krog may have ruined villages, but it was nothing compared to what Sparr would do.

As the sled approached the gate, the children saw a blaze of blue wizard light and heard the sound of swords being drawn.

Errck! The sled stopped before the city walls.

Queen Relna, Lunk, and Smee were there, together with King Zello and the wizard Galen.

"Keeah, children, sir!" boomed Galen's deep voice, looking the Prince of Stars up and down. "Zello and I came as soon as we could. Wraiths are gathering for a charge on the city!"

"They shall not win," said Queen Relna.

Eric looked at Keeah, then turned to Neal and Julie at his side. He felt his heart race. "Guys, we have the power to do this together."

A smile drifted across the prince's lips. "And now is the right time to use it —"

"Us first!" boomed Rolf. Together with his Silversnow friends, the knight gave his great shield a shove and they all jumped on.

Gathering speed, the three friends tilted to the left and — *vrrm!* — plowed through the first line of wraiths, toppling them like bowling pins!

Thwapp-app! Max, Julie, and Neal flung snowball after snowball and got the wraiths before they could stand.

Galen laughed. "Now us!" He leaped forward, his fingers blasting. The sky over Jaffa City went bright with sparks as he and Keeah and Eric pushed the wraiths back to the Farne Woods.

"And now, for him," said Relna. "Look there!"

High in the clouds was a dark, twisted shape, weaving and diving toward the city.

It was the terrible Golden Wasp. On its back was none other than Lord Sparr. The scar on his forehead from when the Wasp stung him long ago was glowing bright red.

"If it isn't the creep himself," said Neal.

"And his icky pet, too," added Julie.

The Wasp veered down at them, shrieking and buzzing. Its deadly tail was arched to strike.

Eric shuddered. "It's huge!"

A howl of laughter came from the sky. "If you mean me," snarled Sparr loudly, "then you're quite right! I *am* huge! And soon to be huger, without Jaffa City to worry about! And, by the way, Keeah, thanks for the sound track!"

Plimmm! He plucked Keeah's harp

with his bony fingers and the Wasp shot up into the sky.

"I can't stand it!" shouted Keeah. "He can't have the harp. He can't have more power!"

"And he won't," said the prince. "When I heard the wraiths hissing, I knew some of Krog remains in me. The Wasp needs a foe. A monster must battle — a monster!"

As they watched, the Prince of Stars began to change shape back into the spiky-winged beast.

A moment later — *roooorrr!* — Krog loomed before them again.

With a great flap of his wings, the prince lifted into the air. "Eric, I need your power. Care to join me?"

Without thinking, Eric looked at Julie. "Um?"

"You got it!" She took his hand and flew up.

Eric slid onto the prince's scaly back. A moment later, they shot high into the air.

Zzzzz! The Golden Wasp turned to him.

Sparr hissed, "A boy and a stranger!"

"And yet, something tells me we've done this before!" the prince said, flying closer. "Wasp, meet Krog!"

Sparr's eyes flashed as he plucked the harp. The Wasp buzzed in response, then set its deadly golden eyes on Eric.

"I shall win!" cried Sparr.

"We'll see about that!" yelled the prince.

Howling, Sparr strummed again, and the Wasp dived at Eric and the prince.

10

Star Sparkle

The prince and the Wasp roared across the air at each other, then circled.

Eric kept his eyes glued to the sorcerer.

"Get ready, Sparr!" he whispered.

Sparr had already taken the Coiled Viper. Now he had the Wasp. Eric knew what was next.

The Red Eye of Dawn.

Eric crouched. "We need to get the harp back."

"Moving in," said the prince, flapping his beastly wings and looping nearer to the Wasp.

When Sparr had all three Powers, he would be nearly unbeatable. That's what this was all about. The journey north. Finding Krog. The prince. It was what Galen had told him once.

There is a greater purpose here.

It was about power.

Eric's power to battle Sparr.

"Closer . . ." said Eric. "And . . . now!"

The prince veered over the Wasp, and Eric let go a sudden stunning burst of light — *zzannng!*

"*Eeeoow* — silver sparks —!" Sparr shook from Eric's blast and loosened his grip on Keeah's harp. It fell from his hand.

It was just what Eric wanted. As the prince flew by, Eric flung out his hand.

Thwap! Eric grabbed the magic harp.

"Nooooo!" cried Sparr, staring back at the boy.

In the second that their eyes met, Eric tried to read the mind behind those eyes, the cruel smile, the glowing V-shaped scar on Sparr's forehead.

The sorcerer looked like . . . a monster.

Krog had, too. But the prince's eyes told the truth about him. What did Sparr's eyes tell? Was he the *real* monster?

"Be — gone!" cried the sorcerer. He blasted Eric, knocking him off the prince's back. *Blam! Ka-blam!*

Eric tumbled to the ground, splashing snowflakes everywhere. The harp bounced across the frozen earth to Neal.

"Got it," said Neal. "Keeah, your harp —"

But the princess was busy keeping the wraiths in the forest. "Neal, play it. Play it now!"

"You don't want me to —"

"Play it!" cried Eric, stumbling to his friend.

Neal touched the harp. *Ploink! Splang!*

Suddenly, the Wasp lunged down, then flipped over and back up again.

"*Aaaa-eeee!*" Sparr howled from its back.

"Keep on playing," yelled Keeah. "Pluck the strings!"

Neal grinned and strummed the strings hard. *Ploink! Blang! Blimfff!*

The Wasp spun completely around, then began to buck wildly up and down.

"Silly insect!" cried Sparr, trying to stay on. "Everyone, leave now! Go! To the Dark Lands!"

"If you can!" Galen cheered, sending blast after blast after Sparr. The Wasp, with the sorcerer still clinging tightly, jerked away across the sky.

The wraiths hissed and flitted after their master, black smears against the snow.

"Woo-hoo!" boomed Rolf. "Look at them go!"

A moment later, the sorcerer and his shadow creatures were gone.

"Hooray!" cried Eric, running to Keeah. "We did it! Today, we whooped Sparr!"

Everyone gathered at the city gates.

"Well done, one and all!" said Galen. "Even if we haven't seen the last of Sparr, it's always good to give him a bit of trouble!"

Landing nearby, the Prince of Stars soon turned into himself again. He bowed before the king and queen. "It is an honor to serve you."

Smiling, King Zello extended his large hand. "As man or beast, you are quite a good warrior!"

"And you are welcome to stay," said the queen. "We should like your company."

"I cannot stay," he replied. "Before Krog, I was searching for someone. I must continue the search. But I can't leave without giving a gift."

From the depths of his cloak, the prince pulled out a small dark bottle. "Magically, this old bottle seemed to call out to me from Krog's treasure. I sense it will help against Sparr, but not how we expect!"

Neal sniffed the bottle. "Like if you fill it with stinky stuff and splash it on Sparr, he'll have to change his black suit? Maybe he won't be so scary if he has to wear polka dots!"

As everyone laughed, Keeah turned to the prince. "You said you were searching. For who?"

The prince breathed deeply. "In my mind, I see a small child with golden curls dressed all in blue, sitting alone in a silver tree. Until I know who that child is and

what it might mean, I must keep searching."

Saying this, he stepped to the top of a
mound of snow and called out. An instant
later — *fwap* — *fwap* — *fwap!* — Otli,
Jotli, and Motli, his three crows, perched
together on his shoulders.

Standing against the blue-black sky, the
prince whipped his dark cloak about, scattering tiny star-shaped sparks around him —
pling — *bing* — *thoom!*

As everyone watched, this fountain of
light faded. And so did he.

The Prince of Stars was gone.

Galen stared at the spot, then gave out
a sigh. "So! Our strange man resumes his
wanderings once more — if he even *is* a
man. It's odd, but I feel I've known him
forever."

"Me, too," said Eric.

Keeah nodded. "I think we'll see him again."

Relna turned to Eric. "Thank you for your powers today. We shall need them again."

"Keeah showed me how to control them," said Eric. "Maybe I won't break any more dishes!"

The queen laughed. "And Julie . . . keep secret those paintings of Droon. But do not stop making them. They are very special."

Julie beamed. "Thank you. I'll be careful."

Whoosh! A glow appeared nearby. The rainbow stairs glimmered near the walls.

Neal sighed. "I guess it's time to go home."

"It's back to the ice caves for us," said Rolf, shoulder to shoulder with Lunk and Smee. "We'll return treasure to everyone who lost it."

"We'll put it in sacks and use the prince's big sled to carry us around," said Lunk.

"Ho-ho!" said Smee. "People will love us!"

The knights waved, climbed into the sled, then rode away over the hills.

"It's time for us, too," said Galen, clutching the prince's bottle in his hand. "To plan for Droon's future, now that Sparr has the Wasp."

"And keep him from stealing any more power," chirped Max, scampering to the wizard's tower.

Keeah gave her friends one last hug. "This means me, too. Good-bye. Until next time!"

Waving, the three friends trotted up the shimmering stairs. At the top, they looked out Eric's basement window and saw the neighborhood kids sledding in the snowstorm.

"We did some sledding today," said Julie, closing the closet on the purple clouds of Droon.

"In the North!" Neal boomed with a laugh.

Eric thought of the prince's bright eyes. Then of Sparr's dark, terrifying ones.

Shaking his head, he gazed at the storm outside. "I was thinking," he said. "Powers are cool, but maybe this snow is . . . you know . . ."

"Just good plain snow?" said Julie, heading for the stairs. "There's really only one way to find out —"

Without another word, the three friends raced one another out the back door and leaped into a world of drifting, swirling, spinning flakes of snow.

ABOUT THE AUTHOR

Tony Abbott is the author of more than fifty funny novels for young readers, including the popular *Danger Guys* books and *The Weird Zone* series. Since childhood he has been drawn to stories that challenge the imagination, and, like Eric, Julie, and Neal, he often dreamed of finding doors that open to other worlds. Now that he is older — though not quite as old as Galen Longbeard — he believes he may have found some of those doors. They are called books. Tony Abbott was born in Ohio and now lives with his wife and two daughters in Connecticut.

For more information about Tony Abbott and the continuing saga of Droon, visit www.tonyabbottbooks.com.

THE SECRETS OF DROON

by Tony Abbott

Under the stairs,
a magical world awaits you!